Alligator Afternoon

Written by Nikki Lund
Illustrated by Nicolas Peruzzo

ISBN 978-1-61225-379-4

Published by Mirror Publishing
Fort Payne, Alabama 35967

Printed in the USA.

For Philip & Colin – my first audience and the
inspiration for many a story about Peter.
With special thanks for all the support to Randy, Annie, and Natalie.

May we all never lose our ability to imagine.

"Push the button," said his mom as they got into the elevator on the 19th floor.

"Ooh-kaay," said Peter slowly. He hated going grocery shopping. He would rather be playing or reading a book in his apartment – anything but going grocery shopping.

The elevator doors opened. This certainly wasn't the first floor. It was very strange. Everything looked flat. It was as if he was looking out at a picture in a book.

He took a step out of the doors. Everything still looked flat. He looked down at himself – he was not flat. He looked back into the elevator – it was empty!

"That's odd," he thought. He didn't have time to think about it any longer because a boy - a flat looking boy! - raced up to him. "Come on, hurry up."

"What?" said Peter.

"Come on, hurry up!" the flat boy said again. "Do hurry. My alligator is in trouble. I need your help."

Peter looked up at the boy again. The boy looked so flat that if you looked at him from the side he was no thicker than a sheet of paper. But all Peter said was, "Alligator?"

"Yes, my pet alligator, Al. Do hurry! He's this way. I hope we're not too late."

The boy led the way down a flat path through the flat woods. Now Peter could hear running water.

They came to a river.

"This way, come on – go faster! Hurrreee!"
Peter saw a bridge in the distance.
"Almost there," the boy said.

And then Peter saw it. An alligator holding on tight to the post of the wooden bridge. The water was rushing past him and he looked very scared.

"I don't think I can hold on much longer, Tyler," the alligator shouted.

"We're going to save you, Al," Tyler shouted back. "Quick, Peter, how can we save him?"

Peter looked all around him but couldn't see anything that could be helpful. He looked further away and saw a long branch that had fallen from a tree. "Follow me," he said.

Tyler and Peter ran to the branch. The branch was too heavy for them to lift.

"Oh no," they said together.

Peter rolled his eyes. And, as he did, he saw it – a long vine hanging from the next tree. That might work. Could they pull it down?

"Grab it and pull when I count to three."

"One ... two ... three!"

They pulled and pulled. The vine came crashing down to the ground. Birds flew up all around and scared them for a moment.

Dragging the vine behind them they ran back to the bridge.
Now what?

They put one end of the vine in the water and let it out, but it floated down river past the alligator, out of his reach.

"Oh no," they said together.

They pulled it back. Al wasn't saying anything now; in fact, he was looking very tired.

Peter grabbed the vine again and ran up the riverbank away from Al.

"Don't go," said Tyler.

"I'm not," said Peter. "You'll see. Come and help."

Tyler ran up as Peter let one end of the vine down into the river again. He slowly let out more and more. Tyler held on too.

The vine got caught in the river current and floated down under the bridge – straight to Al.

As Al grabbed hold the boys pulled hard, slowly bringing him to the riverbank. Al managed to climb up a little bit and then flopped down. He was very pale and tired out.

"Thank you, oh thank you," cried Tyler. "You saved Al! How can I thank you?"

"Can you show me the way out? My mom must be getting worried by now."

"Oh, yes, follow the path and you will see the elevator straight ahead. Just push the button".

Peter said goodbye and was happy to see Al with a bit more of his color back.

Following the path, Peter came to the elevator doors and pushed the button.

Ping. The doors opened. He walked in. Everyone looked normal – not flat. No one seemed surprised to see him.

Phew. He smiled to himself.

His mom said, "Push 19 for us please Peter; and can you manage to carry one of these bags?

By the way, how did your shirt get so wet?"

CPSIA information can be obtained
at www.ICGtesting.com
Printed in the USA
BVOW11s1038160817
492168BV00003B/22/P